Other books in the SWITCH series:

Anaconda Adventure

Ali Sparkes

illustrated by
Ross Collins

OXFORD
UNIVERSITY PRESS

OXFORD
UNIVERSITY PRESS

Great Clarendon Street, Oxford OX2 6DP

Oxford University Press is a department of the University of Oxford.
It furthers the University's objective of excellence in research, scholarship,
and education by publishing worldwide in

Oxford New York

Auckland Cape Town Dar es Salaam Hong Kong Karachi
Kuala Lumpur Madrid Melbourne Mexico City Nairobi
New Delhi Shanghai Taipei Toronto

With offices in

Argentina Austria Brazil Chile Czech Republic France Greece
Guatemala Hungary Italy Japan Poland Portugal Singapore
South Korea Switzerland Thailand Turkey Ukraine Vietnam

Oxford is a registered trade mark of Oxford University Press
in the UK and in certain other countries

British Library Cataloguing in Publication Data
Data available

ISBN: 978-0-19-2732408
1 3 5 7 9 10 8 6 4 2

Printed in Great Britain

Paper used in the production of this book is a natural,
recyclable product made from wood grown in sustainable forests.
The manufacturing process conforms to the environmental
regulations of the country of origin.

Photograph on page 127: Thanks to Tiny Drury, cool chameleon.

For Tobey Cole

With grateful thanks to
John Buckley and Tony Gent of
Amphibian and Reptile Conservation
for their hot-blooded guidance on
SWITCH's cold-blooded reptile heroes.

Danny and Josh and Petty

Josh and Danny might be twins but they're NOT the same. Josh loves getting his hands dirty and learning about nature. Danny thinks Josh is a nerd. Skateboarding and climbing are way cooler! And their next-door neighbour, Petty, is only interested in one thing . . . her top secret SWITCH potion.

Danny

- FULL NAME: Danny Phillips
- AGE: 8 years
- HEIGHT: Taller than Josh
- FAVOURITE THING: Skateboarding
- WORST THING: Creepy-crawlies and tidying
- AMBITION: To be a stunt man

Josh

- **FULL NAME:** Josh Phillips
- **AGE:** 8 years
- **HEIGHT:** Taller than Danny
- **FAVOURITE THING:** Collecting insects
- **WORST THING:** Skateboarding
- **AMBITION:** To be an entomologist

Petty

- **FULL NAME:** Petty Hortense Potts
- **AGE:** None of your business
- **HEIGHT:** Head and shoulders above every other scientist
- **FAVOURITE THING:** SWITCHing Josh & Danny
- **WORST THING:** Evil ex-friend Victor Crouch
- **AMBITION:** Adoration and recognition as the world's most genius scientist (and for the government to say sorry!)

CONTENTS

Getting Legless

'Slithery, slithery, slithery . . . ' Petty Potts
pushed her face up against the glass, steaming
it up with her breath and bending her nose
sideways.

'She's going wrong again,' muttered Danny.

'Ahem! Who's *she*?' demanded Petty Potts,
stepping away from the glass and shoving her
thick spectacles up the bridge of her nose so
she could glare at him. 'The cat's mother? I was
merely trying to build the excitement.'

'You don't need to build any excitement!'
Josh pointed to the enormous snake on the
other side of the glass. 'You're just about to
SWITCH me and Danny into one of *those*. It
doesn't get more exciting than that!'

'Although we're not sure why you want

to do it *here*,' Danny added. They were in the reptile house at The Wilderness Zoological Park. 'I mean—surely it would be safer to do this SWITCH in the lab?'

'It would,' Petty said. 'But I'm working on a new theory. Will your behaviour patterns be affected if you SWITCH in close proximity to a real snake?'

Josh and Danny stared through the glass and shivered with excitement . . . and a little fear. On the far side a yellow and black scaly face rose up, staring back at them through almond shaped eyes. A black forked tongue waved in the air, trying to scent them.

'A yellow anaconda,' read Danny, peering at the little information plaque next to the display. 'Grows up to two or three metres in length and eats birds, reptiles and mammals. Non venomous. Kills prey by constriction. Not large enough to kill humans. Aaaw!' He turned to Petty. 'I want to be large enough to kill humans! Why can't I be large enough to kill humans? It's not fair.'

Josh thwacked the back of his twin brother's head with a rolled up Wilderness Zoological Park souvenir guide, briefly flattening Danny's spiky blond hair. 'You're not planning to kill any humans, are you? So it's not really a problem!'

'I know . . .' pouted Danny. 'I'd just like to know we could if we wanted to . . .'

'Which is precisely why you're getting this SWITCH spray,' Petty said, holding out a small white plastic bottle with a spray nozzle on the top. The letters 'Y A' for yellow anaconda were written on it in permanent marker. 'I do have a green anaconda spray too, and they're the huge, human-eating size. But that's for later. For now, I don't want you getting over-excited and deciding to crush me to death on a whim. And in any case, you're only going to be SWITCHed for half a minute. This bottle has a very precise spray button and I've calculated the dose for exactly thirty seconds and no more.'

When Josh and Danny had first been SWITCHed it was by accident—into house spiders. It had been utterly terrifying to be the unwitting guinea pigs for Petty's Serum Which Instigates Total Cellular Hijack—and it would never have happened at all if Piddle, their dog, (named after a rather unfortunate habit he had when he got excited) hadn't run into their neighbour's back garden. It was while rescuing him that they'd stumbled into Petty's secret underground laboratory—and right into a jet spray of SWITCH.

Now, months later, it was hard to imagine how they'd resisted getting involved with Petty's SWITCH Project. Since they'd helped her find the missing code to the Reptile SWITCH formula they'd been more and more excited about taking part in the experiments. Being SWITCHed into reptiles was going to be amazing!

Even so, today Josh felt a twinge of worry—a zoological park was a bit public for a brand new SWITCH. 'Are you sure about this?' he asked Petty. 'It will definitely only last thirty seconds?'

'Certain!' Petty said. 'Now—check there's nobody coming and we'll give it a blast.' While Josh and Danny poked their heads out past the door of the reptile house—a humid hexagonal building filled with large glass-fronted displays containing all kinds of exotic cold-blooded creatures—Petty put her bag down on a table in the centre of the room. It was used as an education centre too, so there were tables and chairs and benches along one wall.

'Nope—nobody around,' Danny said, coming back in. 'Good job we're off school on a teacher training day. This place would be full of kids at the weekend.'

'Yes—but school parties sometimes come in too,' Petty said. 'And I saw one back by the entrance gate. Still—if nobody was anywhere near the bottom of the path we know we have a minute or more. It's a long walk up here. So—climb on

the table please. As soon as you SWITCH, pay
attention to the yellow anaconda. Look at it. And
let it look at you. I will be filming to see if there are
any differences in behaviour. And you'll SWITCH
back in half a minute—so no chance to get
chummy with my windpipe!'

Danny and Josh sat cross-legged on the table,
grinning with excitement. They'd been looking
forward to this moment for weeks and weeks—
ever since they'd found the last REPTOSWITCH
cube and Petty had begun working on the new
formula. Josh decided to stop worrying and just
have fun. He fixed his blue eyes on Petty and said
'Ready!' Petty sprayed him in one short burst.
Then Danny.

Three seconds later two yellow anacondas were coiling on the table, black and yellow scales gleaming in the soft light, diamond shaped heads swaying back and forth and black forked tongues flickering in the air.

'YESSSSSSSSSSSSS!' hissed Danny.

'This is SSSSSSSSSO cool!' hissed Josh.

Although it was weird to have no arms or legs, he could feel the immense strength and agility of his sleek body. He lifted his head, feeling the muscles contract and relax in waves just under his beautiful gleaming scales, and rose up majestically to stare at Danny.

'Look at my toooongue!' Danny poked out his forked tongue and waved it around. It was like a tiny snake in itself—strong and agile.

'We're quite small,' Josh said, eyeing his tail. 'About a metre, I think. Not big enough to kill much more than a mouse. Oooh—quick—look at whatsisface! We've only got about ten seconds left.'

Whatsisface, the real anaconda, was now staring at them through the glass with interest.

He'd risen up higher and his tongue was going
crazy . . . but he couldn't hope to get much
information through it, thought Josh. Not with
that thick glass between him and them. Petty's
experiment would have worked better if he and
Danny had been able to get in with the other
snakes, behind the glass. But as anacondas
occasionally ate each other, it was probably just as
well they hadn't.

'How are we talking this time?' asked Danny,
writhing around in great excitement, his scales
rubbing together with a soft whispery noise.

'Oh—like most reptiles—through scent and body language and a bit of hissing,' explained Josh. 'You're smelling through your tongue!' Josh was mad about wildlife and knew a lot of this stuff. 'Ooh—I can't wait to do this back in Petty's garden. We can go into the stream at the back. You know anacondas are brilliant swimmers, don't you? They spend more time in water, in the wild, than on land!'

'Hmmm—but will she let us?' asked Danny. 'Since she's moved her secret lab to the attic above Princessland she's not doing any experiments in the old lab at home any more, is she? In case government spies are watching her!'

'Well . . . we'll just have to go off down the park and have a swim in the lake,' Josh said.

'Um . . . shouldn't we have SWITCHed back by now?' asked Danny. 'It's been more than thirty seconds, hasn't it?'

Josh turned to look at Petty and saw that she was legging it out of the room. 'WRONG SPRAY BOTTLE!' she shouted, as she went. 'GETTING ANTIDOTE FROM CAR! HIDE!' The last they saw of her was the back of her purple beanie hat—and even that looked quite panicky.

'Oh great!' Danny stared back at Josh. 'She's done a runner!'

'We'll be fine.' Josh gulped. 'She'll be back soon. We just have to hide in case anyone else comes in.'

The real anaconda was swaying about even higher now, behind the glass. Its eyes glimmered and its tongue was still dancing. It seemed to be laughing at them.

'Come on . . .' Josh said. 'Get down!'

They worked their way down the table legs, coiling around them to reach the floor. Under the table wasn't a good hiding place. They might easily be seen by someone walking in. 'This way!'

Danny hissed, sliding across the cold tiles and under one of the long wooden benches against one wall of the reptile house. Soon Josh and Danny were hiding in the shadows.

'She won't be long,' Josh said. 'She'll be back any minute. It'll be fine! Hey—I can feel her vibrations now.' And he *could* feel the vibration of steps back up the path outside. Of course, snakes were excellent at picking up vibrations— sometimes from far far away. Josh knew that it was one of the things which helped them hunt.

'Erm . . . isn't that quite a *lot* of vibrations for one genius scientist?' Danny queried.

And then the door crashed open and two dozen sets of feet pounded into the room.

And not one of them was Petty's.

In the Bag

Josh and Danny flattened themselves right against the wall as the stampede thundered across the floor. The shoes were mostly black and shiny with silver buckles across white, lace-trimmed socks. They crashed around in all directions . . . some rushing towards the glass displays, some coming to rest by the tables and some, alarmingly, stomping down right by the benches.

'Girls! Girls!' called a shrill voice. 'Don't forget to make notes on your worksheets!'

It was a school party. A girls' school party. Keeping his head low, Danny could see girls in maroon and grey checked skirts, white blouses and maroon blazers—and straw hats! A proper posh girls' school, then.

'What are we going to do?' he whispered to Josh.

'Just keep very still!' Josh whispered back. 'They won't stay long. There's loads of other things to see around the park. They'll only be here five minutes. And Petty will be back any time . . .'

Danny kept very still. He found it quite easy to keep his reptilian body motionless. And of course, snakes were good at that. Josh had told him they could keep incredibly still—and then strike, out of nowhere. But he couldn't help his tongue continually sliding out from his lipless mouth and flickering in the air. Gathering information through scent glands, according to Josh.

The noise of the girls was head splitting. They were constantly babbling and squeaking and even screaming when they saw a reptile they didn't like the look of. But one girl was sitting quietly on the bench, just above them. Her feet were not moving. Her shoes were spattered with mud. She didn't say anything to any of the others.

'Righto, girls!' said the teacher. 'Let's have our packed lunches while we're here. Sit down and get your food out.' There was another short stampede as the girls rushed to get a decent seat.

'Move up, new girl!' said one of them, in a sneery voice, and the girl sitting above Josh and Danny was shoved abruptly along the bench. She didn't say anything, but she lifted her muddy shoe and stepped down hard on the shiny neat shoe of the girl who'd arrived next to her. The new arrival screamed in a very melodramatic way. 'Miss Biffle! Miiiss! Charlotte just stamped on my foot! Charlotte just broke my toes! Miiiss!'

'Shove me again and I'll make you some toe jam,' promised Charlotte in a sweet voice. Josh and Danny snorted with amusement. They liked the sound of Charlotte.

But the teacher wasn't paying attention amid the racket of twenty-four girls settling down to a picnic. Above their heads Danny and Josh could hear the pop, crackle, and rasp of plastic tubs opening and food being freed from paper or tin foil.

'Oooh look!' said the crushed toe victim. 'Charlotte's got Marmite on white bread again! Is that all you can eat, Charlotte? Oh—and a bag of Wotsits! What a lunch! So yeasty and cheesy . . .'

Several girls tittered around the room.

'Or is that just your disgusting socks?' went on the voice.

There was a small crackle of a packet and then a loud scream. 'Miiiiiss! Miss Biffle!' Amid the new screaming there was also laughter—hoots of it. 'Miiiiisss! Charlotte just stuck two Wotsits up my nose!'

'It's a good look, Isobella,' Charlotte said. 'They match your eyes.' More girls laughed. It looked as if this Charlotte was winning the match.

Josh and Danny were laughing helplessly too, their scaly heads rocking from side to side. They only wished they could have seen it. Miss Biffle called for calm and told Charlotte off and things settled down again.

'I'll get you back for that!' Isobella whispered. 'Just you wait!'

'Whenever you're ready,' Charlotte said.

A few seconds later an orange rolled under the bench. Then a face with a neat blond fringe and two wide grey eyes peered into their hiding place.

And that's when Isobella really started screaming.

'AAAAAAAH! SNAKES! SNAKES! MISS! THERE ARE SNAKES!!'

Immediately there was a mad cacophony of shrieks and yelps and all the feet were running to the far end of the room and jumping up on chairs and tables. 'What do you mean, Isobella?' bellowed Miss Biffle. 'Of course there are snakes in here! It's a reptile house!'

'No! Escaped snakes! Under the bench!' More hysterical shrieking shook the air and the teacher walked hesitantly across to the bench and peered under. She gasped and called out, 'Stay back, everyone! Stay back! Isobella—Jemima! Run and find a member of zoo staff right away.'

'What do we do now?' hissed Danny, the cool blood in his veins pumping hard around his lengthy body as panic started to creep through him.

'Just keep really still!' hissed back Josh. 'And stop hissing!' It was all he could think of . . . and it wasn't much. Any minute a zoo keeper would be along with a snake hook and a bag—and they'd be caught! Unless they SWITCHed back to boys first—and that would also be a catastrophe. How would they ever explain themselves? Petty Potts—of course—was nowhere to be seen.

'What is going on?' A new voice rang out amid all the squeaks and shrieks.

'Oh, Miss Butcher!' breathed Miss Biffle. 'Thank goodness you've come! It's snakes! Under the bench! We're waiting for the staff to come and catch them.'

'Well—shouldn't you be evacuating the girls?' demanded Miss Butcher.

'Oh yes—I suppose so,' agreed Miss Biffle. 'Come on, girls—we'd better wait outside.' And the girls all ran for the door in a heaving mob.

'Girls! Girls!' called Miss Butcher. 'Don't push! It's unladylike. Charlotte! Why are you coming back inside? You've only just gone out!'

'I forgot something, Miss,' came back Charlotte's increasingly familiar voice. And then she was running across the room right towards the spot where Danny and Josh were frozen under the bench. 'My bag!'

'Don't!' shrieked Miss Biffle. 'That's right where the snakes are!'

But Charlotte not only grabbed her bag, she also tipped it over and scrabbled around by the bench, scooping all her bits and pieces back into it. 'It's OK!' she called back. 'They're only small ones. And they're not venomous—they're constrictors. And . . . I have to be honest . . . um . . . they're not real.'

'I beg your pardon!' squawked Miss Biffle.

Then the girl whispered under the bench. 'Quick! Get into my bag! NOW!'

Josh and Danny gaped at each other and then slid right into the open neck of the duffle bag, passing, as they did, some long, thin, rubbery things.

Charlotte dug her hand back into her bag the second they were both coiled up inside it, amid her pens, paper and crumpled up sweet wrappers. She pulled out the long, thin, rubbery things.

'Josh!' whispered Danny. 'Did you see that? Did you?'

'Yes! But shhhhh! We have to stay quiet!' urged Josh.

Danny had seen two amazing things. One was that they had just been replaced, under the bench, by two rubber toy snakes.

The second was that he knew who Charlotte was. And they could not have asked for a better rescuer.

'Charlotte Wexford—what ARE you talking about?' shouted Miss Butcher. 'I demand you tell me this instant!'

'Well . . .' sighed Charlotte. Through a gap at the top of the bag Josh and Danny saw her reach under the bench and pull out the two fake snakes. 'It was kind of a joke . . . that's all. I didn't think everyone would freak out quite so much.'

'You mean to tell me,' spluttered Miss Butcher, 'that you came in here, planning to play a trick on everyone, deliberately, calculatingly, smuggling in two rubber snakes in your bag?'

'Yeah—*rubber* ones!' Charlotte said, picking up her bag and putting it carefully over her shoulder. 'I mean—I'm not going to go around with *real* snakes in my bag, am I?'

In her bag two real snakes grinned at each other.

'I can't believe it!' whispered Danny. 'It's Charlie!'

Charlie About

The face that peered down at them through the opening in the duffle bag had big brown eyes, a cloud of curly black hair and a naughty grin which Josh and Danny had last seen at their adventure camp in the summer holidays. Charlie was the only friend they had who knew about SWITCH.

'Josh! Danny! The teachers have put me back on the coach as a punishment,' Charlie called in a low voice. 'You can come out now! I mean . . . it *is* you two, isn't it?'

'Yess!' hissed back Danny. 'But how on earth did you know?'

Of course, Charlie couldn't work out what he was saying but she seemed to guess. 'I've got no idea what you two are doing in the middle of my school trip, SWITCHed into snakes,' she went on.

'And you nearly got completely caught out this time! The keeper was just running up from the bottom of the path when we all came out of the reptile house.'

Charlie giggled. 'Then I saw her! Petty Potts! Standing there on the path with a little white SWITCH spray bottle in her hands, looking at us as if her bloomers had just caught fire! And in that second I realized what was happening. A pair of escaped snakes under the bench! Petty Potts in the area! It had to be you two! And so I had to think fast—really fast! And guess what? I'd just bought these rubber snakes from the gift shop! Of course, they've been confiscated now,' she sighed.

'She's brilliant! Just brilliant!' Danny said. 'Best girl in the world!'

'Danny,' Josh said. 'We'd better get out of this bag. We could SWITCH back at any minute. It's a nice bag but I don't want to end up wearing it!' Josh lifted his head through the top of the bag and began to slither across Charlie's arm.

'Wow! You are fab!' murmured Charlie, running her fingers along the smooth black and yellow

scales which formed a three-pronged arrow shape
on his head. Josh soon slid across to the spare
seat next to her and Danny began to wind out
of the bag too. 'YEE-OW!' added Charlie. With
some cause. Suddenly an eight-year-old boy was
sprawling across her lap.

'Ahem. Sorry,' Danny said, scrambling off,
looking a little pink.

'Thank you!' Josh said, also back in boy form
now. 'So much! If you hadn't come along and
swapped those toy snakes for us, we'd be in
captivity now. Behind glass. Probably with one of
the real anacondas deciding which one of us to
crush first.'

'Glad to be of service.' Charlie beamed. 'After all—you helped *me* out back at summer camp. I still can't believe I got to be a frog! It was the best thing ever!'

'What happened to your hair?' Danny asked. In summer camp, where he and Josh had first met Charlie, she'd had her black hair in many long beaded plaits.

'Oh—that!' Charlie tugged at the bloom of frizzy black curls with a frown. 'St Gwendoline's doesn't allow hair with beads in. I had to have them all taken out—and now I have to brush my hair every day! Can you believe it? Me?'

'It still looks cool,' Danny said. 'But you don't like St Gwendoline's much do you?'

Charlie shrugged. 'Mum thought it might calm me down, you know . . . being in a posh school where you have to wear a proper uniform and all that. With strict teachers and . . . eurgh! Straw hats! But it's not that bad . . . most of the girls are all right . . . apart from Isobella!'

'Did you really stick Wotsits up her nose?' chuckled Danny.

'She had it coming,' sniffed Charlie. 'Next time it'll be NikNaks down her knickers!'

'We should probably try to find Petty,' sighed Josh when they'd all finished laughing. 'She'll be getting worried.'

'Doesn't stop her, though, does it?' Charlie said. 'What have you been SWITCHed into since we were all frogs in the summer?'

Danny counted on his fingers, 'Um . . . common lizard and sand lizard . . . chameleons . . . leatherback turtles and—just last week—geckos!'

'Geckos!' echoed Charlie, her face awash with first awe and then envy. 'Ooooh! I would *love* to be a gecko! Did you walk up walls?'

'Yup!' Josh said. 'And across ceilings!'

'I have got to get some of that spray from Petty!' Charlie said. 'It's brilliant that you found those cubes and got the REPTOSWITCH formula for her.'

'That's not all we've found,' Josh said, more seriously now. He and Danny exchanged glances.

'What? What's going on?' asked Charlie.

'We've been getting marbles . . .' explained Danny. 'Or rather clues to find them. Sent to us or delivered in some way.'

'Who from?' asked Charlie.

'That's just it . . . we don't know. We call him— or her—The Mystery Marble Sender,' Josh said. 'We've followed the clues and found four of them now.'

Charlie shrugged. 'Well . . . marbles are no big deal. I've got bags of them at home. Why would anyone bother?'

'They're not ordinary marbles,' Josh said. 'They contain code, like the REPTOSWITCH cubes. Petty Potts's code!'

Charlie looked confused. 'Umm . . . so is *Petty Potts* sending the clues to find SWITCH marbles to you? And . . . er . . . why?'

'No!' Danny said. 'She says she isn't. She's just as confused as we are. She recognized the marble we showed her right away but said she'd forgotten she'd made it. We think it's for a kind of MAMMALSWITCH.'

Charlie's eyes widened. 'What . . . like tigers and elephants and all that?' she murmured.

'Maybe,' Josh said. 'But there are still two more to find before we can give Petty the whole code—and in the meantime . . . it's kind of creepy. Who's sending them to us? And why? What do they know about SWITCH and Petty? And what are they going to do next?'

'Whoever it was even followed us on holiday to Cornwall,' added Danny. 'They sent us a clue on a parachute! We found that marble in a ruined fort just off the coast.'

'Ooooow! I wish I'd been there!' Charlie folded her arms and huffed. 'You two have the best fun!'

'Yeah—and nearly get ripped apart by hungry owls; dropped from a great height; drowned while trapped in fishing net; forced to be gladiators by crazed princesses . . .' listed Danny.

'Sheeesh!' Charlie raised an eyebrow. 'Crazed princesses . . . that does sound scary.'

'Thing is . . . whoever this is . . . are they watching us now?' murmured Josh.

They were all quiet for a while, glancing around them uneasily, and then Charlie went on, 'Anyway . . . is there any chance Petty might let me have just a little gecko SWITCH spray? Or snake SWITCH spray? I'd love to be a snake! I'd love to be a DUCK!'

'A duck?' Josh looked confused. 'You want to be a duck?'

'NO! DUCK!' yelled Charlie. 'Miss Butcher's coming!'

Josh and Danny threw themselves into the aisle, crawled at top speed towards the back of the coach and hid behind the seats—just in time. The coach door opened and Miss Butcher strode in.

'Charlotte Wexford!' she barked. 'I'm afraid you have to come with me. As much as I would like to leave you here on your own all afternoon, we are heading down to the river walk now and health and safety rules mean I can't leave you unsupervised. Although it's certainly what you deserve for your appalling behaviour.'

'Yes, Miss Butcher,' Charlie said. She didn't sound remotely troubled.

'You can wipe that cheerful look off your face, too,' snapped Miss Butcher. 'You needn't think, just because I have to bring you along, that you're about to have any fun. You'll stay right between Miss Biffle and me the whole time. And I will call your mother into the school to discuss your future just as soon as we get back today.'

Charlie sighed. 'Yes, Miss Butcher,' she said, getting to her feet and managing to sound a bit less chippy.

'I really don't know what gets into you,' muttered the teacher, stepping out of the coach. 'You're easily as clever as the other girls but you're always so naughty.'

'I'm not really naughty,' Charlie was saying as the coach door closed. 'I'm just misunderstood . . .'

Danny got up from behind the seat and peeped out of the window as the teacher and their friend walked away. 'It's not fair,' he said. 'Charlie got herself into big trouble—just to save you and me! And now she's going to get into even more trouble when they call her mum in. What if she gets expelled? It'll be our fault—and Petty's fault too.'

'There must be something we can do,' Josh said. 'But I can't think what. We can't tell them that Charlie was actually saving our lives. Nobody would believe us.'

'No . . .' sighed Danny. 'Being SWITCHed is amazing, like having super powers. But how much good is it? Charlie's doomed. There's nothing we can do . . .'

Pocket Problem

Petty was worried. Really worried. Josh and Danny might imagine that she was a heartless scientist, obsessed only with her own success, but she really did care about what happened to them. After all . . . who else was going to help her with her experiments if Josh and Danny got eaten?

Of course, if they were still in anaconda form it was highly unlikely that anything *would* try to eat them . . . but a panicky member of the public might stamp on them or the keeper might catch them and put them in with another constrictor and it might . . . Petty shuddered, imagining two Josh and Danny shaped bumps moving slowly down the body of the huge green anaconda she'd seen in the reptile house. This breed had been known to eat each other—*and* small humans. So, SWITCHed or unSWITCHed, Josh and Danny could be lunch.

There had been no sign of them in the reptile house, and the keeper, coming out past her as she went in, had not been carrying a bag of captured snakes. So where had Josh and Danny gone? She'd searched for them in the zoo shop, the café, even in the small Chatz TV marquee which was set up near the penguins, recording some kind of wildlife programme. Josh would love that! But he wasn't there.

She could see that party of schoolchildren—a posh girls' school by the look of the straw hats—heading along the path towards the river. She hurried towards them and called out, 'Have any of you seen two boys—blond—twins—about your age?'

The girls looked at each other and then back at her. Some of them shrugged and several of them giggled. 'I love her hat!' sniggered one girl with a shiny fair bob of hair and a superior expression. 'It's soooo antique.'

Petty narrowed her eyes at the girl as she patted her battered beanie. 'Well, I'd offer to swap it for yours,' she said. 'Except your head is far too small.

Such a tragedy, an undersized brain!'

'Well! I've never been so insulted!' gasped the girl.

'Really?' said Petty. 'I'm surprised nobody's made the effort.'

Another girl, with a cloud of black curls and dark brown eyes, hooted with laughter and gave Petty a little wave as the party was hurried along the path by its two guardian teachers. The laughing girl was walking close to the teachers. They were deep in conversation with each other and paying no attention to her as she turned back to Petty and motioned urgently at her . . . as if she wanted Petty to follow.

Uncertainly, Petty followed, keeping a short distance from the school party. Then the girl dropped down and started to fiddle with her shoe. Her teachers, calling out to their pupils ahead to make notes of the trees along the river, didn't notice.

Petty caught up and the girl immediately bounced up on her feet and gave her a friendly punch on the shoulder. 'Petty! It's meeee! Charlie!'

'Good gracious!' Petty squinted through her smeary glasses. 'So it is! Whatever happened to your hair?'

'Never mind that now,' Charlie said. 'We haven't got long! Josh and Danny are OK. I rescued them in my bag. I had to leave them on the school coach, though, hiding.' She waved back towards the zoo car park.

'Thank heavens for that!' sighed Petty, turning to go.

'But wait . . . can't I have just a little SWITCH spray before you go? Pleeeeease?' Charlie gave Petty the big eyes treatment. 'I mean . . . I did just save Josh's and Danny's lives! Probably!'

'And I thank you very much,' Petty said. 'But I don't hand out SWITCH like Smarties, you know. Well . . . I did once, but that was a bad idea . . .'

'But I'd be ever so careful!' insisted Charlie. 'I would never use it in public or . . .'

'Charlie! You are a first rate girl and I would love to get you on the SWITCH Project,' Petty said. 'But I'm not handing over SWITCH spray to you just for fun. You know how dangerous it is. Didn't you nearly end up as a heron's breakfast last time? No—I'm sorry, but that's that.'

And Petty turned on her heel and fell over.

'Oooh—these stupid woodland paths!' she snapped, as Charlie helped her to her feet. 'What's wrong with a nice bit of tarmac?' And, carefully stepping over the tree root which had tripped her, Petty hurried away.

Charlie was about to call after her. She really *was*. Because a small white bottle with a squirty spray button on it had fallen out of Petty's coat pocket as she tripped. Charlie really *wouldn't* have kept it if Miss Butcher hadn't, at that moment, turned round and bellowed at her from further along the path.

'Charlotte Wexford! Come here AT ONCE!'

'Oh well,' muttered Charlie, slipping the bottle into her blazer pocket. 'I'll be able to post it to her. Probably.'

Josh and Danny hit the emergency exit button and got off the coach at the back, without getting noticed. Happily, it didn't set off any kind of alarm. A minute later they found Petty Potts stomping up to the car park, muttering to herself.

'It's OK—we're safe,' called Josh.

'You'll never guess what!' called Danny, as they reached Petty on the path to the car park. 'We were rescued by—'

'Charlie Wexford!' Petty said. She seemed to be turning out her pockets. 'Yes, I know. I just met her on the river path. And I do believe the little lightfingers pick-pocketed my SWITCH spray!'

'What—Charlie? Steal? She wouldn't do that!' Josh said.

'Don't be so sure,' sniffed Petty. 'She's a very determined young lady and she wanted some SWITCH.'

'Even so,' Danny said. 'Charlie's all right!'

'I didn't say she wasn't all right,' Petty said. 'I've been known to steal things myself when it was desperately important. But not just for fun! Come on—we have to find her and get that spray back.

There's been far too much upset today. Why on earth did you think it would be a good idea for us to try out a SWITCH at the zoo?'

'We didn't!' Josh said, stonily. 'You did!'

'I did not!' Petty turned and stomped back into the park again and they hurried along with her.

'You did!' Danny said. 'You said you wanted to see how SWITCHing near real snakes affected us.'

'Yes, of course I did!' Petty said. 'So why did you say I didn't?'

'Petty, you could have some amazing arguments just on your own,' sighed Josh.

They saw Charlie, at a distance, down by the river with the other St Gwendoline's following the river wildlife walk. 'We'll run ahead,' Danny said. 'Make sure she doesn't get away!' He and Josh took off, leaving Petty grumbling as she marched on after them, looking out for trippy tree roots.

'Get that SWITCH spray back!' she called after them. 'Charlie has no idea how dangerous it can be! If she uses it there will be trouble. Desperate trouble . . .'

Desperate Trouble

Charlie caught up with the others as they reached the river, which wiggled through the many acres of the zoological park, passing the enclosures of giraffe and rhino and ostrich. At this end, though, it had left the exotic animals behind and was rushing into the countryside. Little information posts along the path offered tips on where to spot woodpeckers, kingfishers, and foxes.

They stopped near an arched stone bridge which spanned the river. Below, on the near side, the water tumbled over some rocks in a small, fast waterfall and on the far side the current moved much faster as the river deepened and flowed on downstream. There were warning signs that nobody should swim in it.

'I haven't got a small head—have I?' Isobella was demanding.

Her two best friends, Lucy and Jemima, chorused, 'Of course not!'

'But that horrid, ugly old witch lady said I had!' pouted Isobella, taking off her straw hat and patting her hair anxiously. 'She said I had an undersized brain!'

'She got *that* right,' muttered Charlie.

Isobella spun round and glared at her. 'What would you know, Wexford?' she spat. Then she turned back to her friends. 'It's horrible! Our teachers should complain to the park staff. It's not right for ugly old witch ladies to go around picking on well brought up young ladies!'

Charlie snorted as she climbed up onto the parapet of the bridge. 'Oh give it a rest, Isobella. Don't be such a wuss.'

Isobella gasped again. 'Who are you calling a wuss?' she hissed.

'Um . . . that would be you!' Charlie said, walking along the parapet, holding her arms out wide for balance.

'I suppose you think you're so brave!' sneered
Isobella. 'Just because you can walk along the wall
of a bridge!'

'Nope. Just very good at it,' Charlie said. 'I do
gymnastics, remember? I have a good sense of
balance.' She stood on one leg to prove it.

'Oh you really think you're it!' Isobella stared,
with her hands on her hips for a moment, and
then scrambled up on the parapet too.

'Whoa!' Charlie said. 'Don't do that! It's
dangerous.'

'But you're doing it!' Isobella said.

'Yes! Because I'm *good* at this! You're not!'
Charlie said, alarmed. 'You can't even balance
along the kerb! Get off, Isobella! Look—I'm
getting down now. It's too dangerous for me.'
And she hurriedly got back down onto the path.
She glanced around, hoping for a change that one
of the teachers would turn and make Isobella get
down—but neither did. They were studying tree
bark.

'Izzy! Don't!' whimpered Lucy.

'You'll fall!' warned Jemima.

But Isobella was smirking and throwing her
arms out wide and walking, rather shakily, along

the top of the narrow stone wall. Three or four metres below her, the river churned and flowed at high speed.

'Isobella! Please!' Charlie gave up trying to be cool as the girl wobbled along to the middle of the parapet.

'You think I can't make it across, don't you?' Isobella said, glancing defiantly at Charlie.

'No! I know you can. I'm sorry—I was just showing off,' gabbled Charlie. 'You're better than I am . . . just . . . get down!'

'I'll get down when I'm good and ready!' snapped Isobella, waving her arms about.

And then she fell off.

Josh and Danny were just running up to Charlie to quietly get back the SWITCH spray when something astonishing happened. One minute Charlie was walking along the top of the parapet (which did not surprise Josh and Danny one bit) and the next minute another girl had got up, wobbled along it, and then fallen off.

The girls watching her, Charlie included, were so shocked they didn't even scream. They just gaped and then ran to the wall and peered over.

Josh and Danny arrived next to them in time to see a straw hat bob up on the surface and spin away downstream. Charlie turned to them, her eyes wide. 'She fell!' she whispered. 'She FELL!' The other girls had begun to react now. They ran to the teachers, screaming.

'I'm going after her!' Charlie said, hauling herself up on the parapet. 'It's my fault!'

'Charlie—no!' hissed Danny. 'It's too dangerous!' And as he said this he saw the blond-haired girl whizzing away downstream, her upturned face pink and shocked. 'You'll never catch up with her and save her! None of us could. We'd need to be superhuman!'

Josh caught his breath and then plunged his hand into Charlie's blazer pocket. He brought out the SWITCH bottle. It was different to the one Petty had used on them earlier—it had the letters G A on it. Josh knew exactly what those letters stood for.

He grabbed Charlie's and Danny's hands and dragged them around the far end of the bridge and down the steep woody slope to the river. Hidden by trees and bushes, Josh knew what they had to do. 'Superhuman no,' he said. 'But super-reptile, yes!' And he sprayed Danny and Charlie and himself.

Seconds later, three enormous green anacondas slid into the river and began to swim downstream.

Current Fun

Josh couldn't believe how fast he was moving. He seemed to have become part of the river; his long, muscular body rippling through the fast flowing water. His eyes and nostrils were positioned on his head at just the right place to stay clear of the bubbling, churning surface. Water weed and bits of twig and leaf rafted along beside him. A low branch touched the surface, speeding towards his head, and he instinctively ducked under. At once his world went pale green and a strange booming gurgle resounded through his head. Then—three seconds later—he was back on the surface.

'Where is she?' he heard Charlie shout.

'I can see her!' Josh called back, although he couldn't see Isobella that well. He could, however, smell her—and sense her body heat. She was struggling along in the water, repeatedly going under and popping up again, about ten metres ahead of them.

'There she is!' Danny called out, spotting a flash of white lacy sock. Although, Josh realized, Danny wasn't really calling out. He was hissing a bit, yes, but like many of the creatures he and Danny had been SWITCHed into, there was other stuff going on which made up their communication. Scent and body language and a bit of telepathy.

Charlie struck ahead and Josh marvelled at what he saw in the water. She was bigger than he and Danny—in the wild, many female snakes were bigger than males. Charlie was at least four metres long! Her scales were green with black pebbly markings along the top. Josh was very glad Petty's second SWITCH spray had been for a green anaconda. There was nothing in the reptile world which could swim faster down a river than a green anaconda.

They were all closing in on Isobella now— but it wasn't looking good. Just ahead of them was another waterfall. From where they were swimming, Danny couldn't see the other side of the drop but there was mist and spray rising up from it. He could hear, too, the sound of water dashing hard onto rocks.

'She'll go over the waterfall!' cried out Charlie. 'Come on!' She powered through the river, carving a deep wake in the water behind her. Josh and Danny shot after her. Working his body left and right in undulating pulses, Danny felt his reptilian heart pounding. At least he thought that was his reptilian heart. He had no idea where a snake kept its heart . . .

Up ahead, Isobella was waving one feeble hand out of the water. Her face was going under again. Charlie could see her eyes were shut. Probably just as well, she thought. It won't help if she sees three huge snakes coming after her! But were they too late? With one immense effort she lunged forward. Now Isobella was seconds away from the drop. How could Charlie save her? How was she going to grab her? Even as she thought this, Charlie opened up her powerful jaws, revealing not just fangs but two rows of needle sharp white teeth, which pointed backwards into her cavernous red mouth.

Upstream, Josh and Danny saw Charlie's jaws open in an amazingly wide gape. Josh remembered that anacondas could literally unhinge their jaws to swallow their prey whole. It was the weirdest thing he'd ever seen. A second later, Charlie had grabbed Isobella's foot in her jaws. The girl was barely conscious now as the giant snake snagged her shoe.

But the danger wasn't over. Charlie had held Isobella back from the waterfall but she was being dragged towards it herself. Her incredibly strong scaly body was rippling hard against the current, desperately trying to pull Isobella back up river, but she was losing the battle. Josh and Danny had to do something—NOW!

Danny flung himself across the powerful current to the nearest bank and whipped his tail across a low branch, wrapping it round and pulling tight. And even as he did this, Josh was wrapping his tail round Danny's upper body, anchoring himself firmly with a tight coil of snake muscle.

'Behind you!' he yelled at Charlie and she glanced back and flipped her own tail round his neck. She tightened it quickly and the whole weight of her body—plus Isobella's—plus the strong pull of the current—dragged against Josh's neck.

'Eeeerm . . . could you just . . . loosen off a bit?' he gurgled. There was very little space left for air to get through.

'Sorry!' Charlie called back. 'But we've got to get back to the bank!'

Danny was taking care of this. He wound his tail round and round the tree branch, steadily dragging himself—and Josh and Charlie and Isobella—back to the bank. A minute later they all flopped onto the ground, exhausted.

Charlie unlocked her jaws from Isobella's soggy school shoe. The thick soles had a row of punctures in them. 'Good job I didn't grab her leg or her arm,' she said. 'I'd have bitten right through it.'

'Is she alive?' Danny asked, slithering across to peer anxiously at the soaking wet schoolgirl.

In response, Isobella coughed, spluttered, rolled over and spat water all over the bank. Then she slumped down again and let out a long sigh. Her eyes were closed. She seemed to be asleep.

The three anacondas looked at each other. What now?

'If she sees us she'll freak out,' Charlie said. 'Probably run right back into the river in panic. We'd better get away. Wow! You two look amazing!' Charlie lifted her head and swayed it from side to side, flickering a black forked tongue out towards Josh and Danny.

'So do you,' said Josh. This was truly the most magnificent creature he'd ever been SWITCHed into. He noticed the orangey-yellow stripes streaking out behind Charlie's and Danny's round dark brown eyes, and the beautiful black and yellow spots along their browny-green bodies. They were all perfect specimens. He and Danny were a little smaller and shorter than Charlie, but not by much. Josh wanted to climb up into a tree and see how strong he was. He wanted to swim some more too—a lot more! He wanted to unhinge his jaws like Charlie had and see how wide they went and what it felt like.

'We should change back any second now,' he sighed. 'Probably just as well—listen!' Above the hiss and bubble of the waterfall they could hear shrill cries as Isobella's teachers rushed along the bank of the river. 'We've got to go!'

'Isobella! Charlie!' called the desperate teachers, getting closer. Any minute now they could spot the astonishing sight of one half-drowned pupil and three huge anacondas coiled on the opposite bank. Josh realized it would look suspiciously as if they were planning a feast of Riverwashed Schoolgirl on a Bed of Woodland Salad. It was time to go.

'Quick—over here!' Danny said, and they all slithered away from the river and made for the cover of the wood. Shady ferns helped to hide them from view as the rescuers came running along the bank.

Charlie lost no time in heading up a tree. She wound herself round the trunk and got above ground quickly, before looping her impressive four metre length along a moss covered branch.

'Isobella! Charlotte!' called more voices. Miss
Biffle and Miss Butcher were bashing their way
along the river bank. At this moment Charlie
SWITCHed back. She fell out of the tree with a
splash, right into the shallows of the river.

'Ugh!' She crawled out and back over to
Isobella. 'Isobella!' she said, shaking the girl by
the shoulder. 'Izzy! Wake up! Stop looking so
drowned!'

Isobella spluttered again and opened her eyes.
She fluttered her lashes and whimpered. 'Don't
be so dramatic,' said Charlie. 'You only fell in a
river and got swept downstream and almost over
the edge of a waterfall!' She grinned. 'We've had
scarier experiences in the school canteen!'

'Charlotte! Isobella!' Shouts of delight and relief could be heard as Miss Biffle and Miss Butcher fought their way along the bank towards them. 'Oh! Thank heavens!' cried Miss Biffle. 'Are you all right?'

'Fine!' Charlie said. 'Just went for a little swim in the river.' She beamed and wrung out a soggy bunch of black curls. 'Although Isobella tried to drink most of it.'

Isobella sat up looking pale and filled with amazement. 'Did you . . . just save my life?' she gasped.

Charlie shrugged. 'Well, I suppose I did,' she said. She'd had help, of course, but nobody would believe she'd had a couple of superhero anaconda sidekicks, so she thought it best not to mention it.

'Charlotte dived in after me and saved my life!' squeaked Isobella as soon as the teachers got there. 'She's a heroine! Charlotte! How can I ever thank you?'

'Ummmm . . . stop dissing my Wotsits?' suggested Charlie.

Twiglet, Anyone?

Beep. Beep. Beep. Beep.

Petty Potts reached the ash tree and peered up at Josh and Danny in its branches.

'That's a lot of top quality snakeskin you're ruining with moss stains.' She waved the small, beeping, black torch-like thing at them. 'At least a dozen handbags' worth.' She turned off the SWITCHee detector. Its blue light went out and the beeping stopped. 'Come on. Get down before you fall down. You're not even a tree climbing breed—you shouldn't be up there! Now, I have some antidote here but I'm not climbing up a tree with it.'

Josh and Danny reluctantly slithered back down. They had enjoyed being snakes immensely. They'd both had a go at making their jaws unhinge and found that they could probably swallow a small computer console each if they wanted to. Or possibly Piddle, their dog. They had also enjoyed watching, from a distance, as Charlie was hailed a heroine by the two teachers for saving Isobella's life. 'Looks like she might not get expelled after all,' Danny had hissed.

Petty held up the spray, but paused long enough to remark, 'Well! That's my best SWITCH yet! I really have done wonders this time.' Then she squirted them with antidote.

'Here you go,' Josh said, pulling the green anaconda SWITCH spray out of his pocket and handing it back to Petty. He was glad he'd shoved it into his pocket just in time, so it had safely SWITCHed too, along with all his clothes, into snakeskin, he guessed. 'It was a good job Charlie did borrow this,' he told Petty. 'If she hadn't had it in her pocket we wouldn't have been able to save that girl who fell in the river.'

'Really?' exclaimed Petty. 'What's happened to Charlie, then?'

'She's SWITCHed back already, and gone back with her teachers,' said Danny. 'Ages ago—even though we all sprayed at the same time.'

'Hmmm,' Petty said. 'Probably to do with mass. She's female so I'm guessing she was much larger.'

'Yeah—she was huge! Amazing!' Danny marvelled. 'She saved that girl from going over the waterfall.'

'Truly?' Petty said. 'Tell me all about it!'

They told her while they made their way back to the car park.

'I have chocolate cake at home,' Petty said, walking to her ancient Morris Traveller car.

'I think chocolate cake will be just the thing to celebrate your life-saving adventure.'

Petty was just about to get in when she spotted an envelope beneath one of the elderly windscreen wipers. Petty snatched it up and opened it. Then she paused, turned and raised her shaggy grey eyebrows at Josh and Danny. Lifting the envelope, she showed them the spiky writing. It read:

JOSH + DANNY PHILLIPS . . . AND THEIR GENIUS FRIEND.

'It seems the Mystery Marble Sender now wants me in the game too,' Petty said. They all stared at each other and Josh felt his heartbeat, not for the first time that day, skip along a little faster.

The note inside read:

DEAR JOSH, DANNY + PETTY
YOU'VE DONE SO WELL YOU SHOULD HAVE NO TROUBLE FINDING THIS MARBLE BEFORE YOU GO.
IT'S A LITTLE STICKY.
REMEMBER, DESTINY AWAITS!

'Is that it?' Danny said. 'The clues are usually better than that!'

'A little sticky?' Josh murmured. 'That could be anything!'

'Wait—there's more,' Petty said. At the bottom was a PS. It read:

DANNY ONLY. OR ELSE THE CLUES—AND YOUR JOURNEY OF DISCOVERY—END HERE.

'Me? Just me?' Danny looked worried. 'But . . . I don't have any idea what the clue means. Why me?'

'Wait—there's more still,' Petty said. She had flipped over the paper and on the back it read:

FISH FINGERS, PEAS, POTATOES, VERRUCA PASTE, GET BEST YELLOW JACKET DRY CLEANED.

'Oh that's just a bit of shopping list,' Danny said. 'We've had that before.'

'Looks like the verruca's not cleared up yet, then,' added Josh.

'OK, everyone!' Danny said. 'What about the clue? What does it mean? What's sticky? And why is it just for me? What am I good at?'

Josh and Petty looked at each other and then back at the zoo. They both had the same expression on their faces. And it was not a good expression.

'Erm . . .' Josh said. 'Maybe it's not to do with what you're good at, Danny.'

'Well . . . why else would the Mystery Marble Sender want me to find this marble?' shrugged Danny.

'Maybe it's something you're really scared of,' Josh said. 'So it's more of a challenge.'

Danny gulped. And then he shook his head and lifted his chin. 'Nothing can be scarier than what we've had to face since we met Petty!' he declared.

'No—of course not!' Josh said, with a weak grin. 'Now . . . something . . . a little sticky. I have an idea.'

Petty nodded. 'So have I,' she said. 'Let's go.'

They re-entered the zoo for the third time that day, waving their day pass tickets at the person on the gate. Josh and Petty immediately headed for a wooden building to their left, ignoring the large pond and the wildfowl area. Danny followed them, puzzled. Something sticky, he thought, might be frog spawn in the pond or something. But no . . .

it was autumn and you didn't get frog spawn in the autumn. Maybe something in the visitor centre sweet shop then . . . but no, this was not a sweet shop. This was . . . this was . . .

'NOOOOOOOOOO!' wailed Danny. 'NOT THE INSECT HOUSE!'

Josh and Petty each grabbed an arm and dragged Danny inside. They knew he was scared stiff of creepy-crawlies and would never go in on his own. It didn't matter that he'd *been* an insect several times; they still freaked him out. It didn't matter that he'd even eaten quite a few insects while he'd been SWITCHed into a reptile or amphibian; he'd blocked that out.

'Why are we here?' whimpered Danny, trying hard not to look at all the many-legged creepy-crawlies in their little glass displays. 'There's nothing sticky about insects, is there? They're all dry and crispy and . . . eurgh!'

'Well, there's nothing sticky about most insects, true,' Josh said, firmly tugging Danny along to a tall, well lit display filled with branches and vegetation. 'Except . . . these.'

Danny looked through the glass and saw branches and vegetation. And twigs. And sticks. Sticks with legs. Sticks . . . with faces.

'NOOOOOOO!' he wailed. 'I HATE STICK INSECTS. They're so CREEPY! NOOOO! This

can't be right! It's another kind of sticky! Toffee!
Yes! Toffee! That's sticky, isn't it? You could hide
a marble in a toffee, couldn't you? You could
definitely—'

Petty tapped him on the shoulder and pointed
into the stick insect display. In the far corner was
a small glass orb with a ribbon of purple running
through it.

It was the latest SWITCH marble. Number five.

Six or seven enormous stick insects were
wiggling about, completely surrounding the
marble.

And only Danny could get it.

Leaf Me Alone

To one side of the stick insect display there was
a small black door with a sign which read STAFF
ONLY. This door should certainly have been
locked—but it was ajar. Petty opened it and pulled
Josh and Danny through with her before any other
visitors or staff could come in and see them. It was
gloomy behind the door. It smelt of warm, damp
vegetation. The hairs on Danny's arms and neck
stood up. His heart was racing. He was here in
the inner sanctum of the INSECT HOUSE! It was
horrific.

Petty had found the back of the stick insect
chamber and was turning a stout plastic peg which
held the access panel in place. Now she was tilting
the panel, allowing a shaft of light and the smell of
warm greenery up through it.

'Come on,' Josh said. 'Breathe in. You can do this.'

'Look,' whispered Danny, standing rigid with his fists clenched at his sides. 'We're twins. Who's going to know the difference if it's you that gets the marble? The Mystery Marble Sender can't see us in here!'

Josh pointed to a little red light in the ceiling. 'Security camera,' he said. 'I think they're watching. But you don't have to. I can get the marble. Even if the Mystery Marble Sender does see us and not send us any more clues, five marbles might be enough for Petty to carry on with creating MAMMALSWITCH.'

'Yes,' Petty said, peering around from the back of the stick insect display. 'I might be able to work it out. After all, there were only six insect and reptile SWITCH cubes. Mostly likely there are only six marbles, too. I might not need the last one . . .'

'But . . . if we're wrong . . .' Danny said. He took a big lungful of air and then let it out in a long, shaky breath. 'No,' he said. 'If we don't get any more clues and you can't work out the formula I'll always know it was my fault. I'll get it.'

Josh clapped his back. 'I *knew* you would!'

Shaking, Danny put his hand through the open panel. In front of him was a network of branches and twigs and leaves. And some of them would be twigs and leaves. And some wouldn't . . .

'Um . . . I think you're going to have to put your head through,' Josh said, close behind him.

Another whimper escaped. Danny knew Josh was right. Without seeing what was below him he could be blindly swiping at stick insects.

'They're quite fragile,' Josh said. 'You'll hurt them—snap their legs off or something—if you grab them.' He was, of course, far more worried about the stick insects than his brother.

Danny slowly pushed his head through the opening, not daring to look up in case of dangling horrors. Below him at least twenty stick insects of all sizes were clambering about. 'Ooooh—they are so hoooorrible!' he moaned.

'They're fantastic!' Josh said, just behind him. 'Their proper name is phasmids. They're even better at camouflage than chameleons. They live on plants. Apart from the praying mantis variety— that's a vicious hunter, that is. And the American

Walking Stick insects can spray stuff out of their glands which can turn you temporarily blind— I'm *going* to *shut up* now . . . ' tailed off Josh, realizing how very unhelpful he was being.

'I'm still going with hoooorrible,' breathed Danny. If he could reach down through the display without the tickle-tickle touch of one of those hideous things against his skin he might just have enough courage left to knock away the thick green one which was crouched right across the marble.

Sweat dripped off his nose. Slowly he moved his hand down, feeling as if he was trapped in a nightmare. Then he felt a tickle. On his left ear. He froze. 'Jo-oo-oosh . . .' he squeaked. 'What's on my ear?'

'Erm . . .' Josh said. 'Nothing. Just a bit of leaf.'

Danny didn't believe him. He started shaking badly and then his hand bumped into a chain of three stick insects, apparently attempting a very slow trapeze act, and they tumbled right across his wrist, waggling their legs and feelers and trying to get a grip.

'Eeeeaaargh!' Danny was ready to freak . . . but he couldn't give up! He just couldn't! He plunged his hand down and flicked the big green one off the marble. He scrabbled, moving the marble three times while yet more stick insects dropped onto his arm. And a leaf was moving down his shoulder. Only it wasn't a leaf. It was a LEAF INSECT— looking all green and leaf shaped and innocent but with LEGS!

'Gaaaaaaaah!' Danny shot back out of the display, desperate to get the creepy-crawlies off him.

'STOP!' Josh yelled. 'Stay ABSOLUTELY STILL!'

Danny froze. Was he about to be blinded by stick insect spit?

Josh gently collected all the creatures clinging to his brother and carefully put them back in the display and closed the panel. 'It's OK—they're all safe!' he sighed.

'THEY'RE all SAFE?' Danny spluttered. 'What about ME? I could have been blinded!'

'Nah—none of these are American Walking Sticks,' Josh said.

'Well, thanks for telling me that NOW!' Danny stared at Josh, twitching.

'Go on,' Josh said. 'Freak. Just do it quietly, OK?'

Danny freaked. Quietly.

'Well done!' Josh said, a minute later when his brother had stopped doing his little dance. 'You were brilliant!' And he gave Danny a rough hug. 'I mean . . . you did get it, didn't you?'

Danny grinned, held out his fist; opened it up.

'Aha!' Petty said, her eyes gleaming in the dim light. 'Number five!'

A Touch of Glass

Back in Petty's lab in the attic above Princessland
(a huge shop filled with stuff for girls, which
was almost as horrifying as stick insects as far as
Danny was concerned), they examined the marble.

'Yes—another hologram—another bit of code,'
confirmed Petty, peering through her powerful
microscope.

Josh and Danny took a look. The hologram this
time was of a cat of some kind. A tabby . . . or a
tiger. It was hard to tell.

Petty looked thoughtful. 'Only one more
to go,' she said. 'So I'm guessing our Mystery
Marble Sender will reveal themselves soon. And
then what? This . . . feels dangerous to me. Very
dangerous.'

'Maybe whoever it is just wants to help,' suggested Danny, with a hopeful shrug.

Petty gave a hollow laugh. 'Ooooh, I doubt that! Nobody ever just wants to help. Everybody's out for themselves! I learned that the hard way when my so-called best friend betrayed me and stole my work (or what he thought was my work) and burnt out my memory!'

She picked up a picture in a shattered glass frame. In it was her old friend, Victor Crouch, his arm around a younger Petty, smiling. He wore a hat but no eyebrows.

'Do you think it *is* Victor Crouch?' asked Josh. 'That he survived being SWITCHed into a cockroach and then found your MAMMALSWITCH code in marbles?'

Petty stared at the picture and narrowed her eyes. 'I'm not sure,' she said. 'It doesn't seem quite like his style. But then . . . maybe I've just forgotten what his style is.'

'Well,' sighed Danny. 'I guess we're going to find out soon, aren't we? It won't be long now before the Mystery Marble Sender isn't a mystery any more.'

'Yes,' agreed Petty. 'But I have a nasty feeling we're not going to like the revelation. Go home now, both of you. Come to the house tomorrow after school. And remember, wherever you go . . . someone is watching!'

Josh and Danny were back home in time for tea, and afterwards they went down the garden with Piddle.

'It's been such a freaky few months hasn't it?' Danny said, as they sat on the grass by the climbing frame and Piddle ran around them, trying to persuade them to throw his ball. 'Nobody would ever believe what's happened to us—that we've been SWITCHed into spiders and all kinds of insects, amphibians and reptiles.'

'Nope,' Josh said. 'But they will one day—when Petty goes on TV. And we'll be part of it. Everyone will know then. We'll be famous.'

'Maybe Charlie will be on TV with us too,' Danny said. 'She ought to be!'

'Danny! Josh!' called Mum, from an upstairs window. 'Get up here now and tidy your room! It's revolting. It's a snake pit! Really!'

DIARY ENTRY 701.2

SUBJECT: MARBLE NUMBER 5

Righto! Let's see if this works. Oooh! It does. I am not typing this. I'm using voice recognition software on my computer. I've always wanted to try this out. I'm speaking these words into a microphone and they're coming out automatically across my computer screen! What fun! Now I can record my diary without using a keyboard . . .

So! Today I took Josh and Danny to the zoo to turn them into anacondas. The experiment went quite well, apart from a slight mix up which left them as snakes for much longer than I inspected. NO—EX-pected. Recognize my voice correctly, you feeble machine! Anyway, after the first SWITCH they were nearly discovered by a school party—but then rescued by none other than Charlie Wexford, our friend from the summer camp! Charlie is very useful. I really must find a way to get her onto the SWITCH project with Josh and Danny.

Anyway—not only that—but my SWITCH formula saved a life today! Josh, Danny and Charlie ended up SWITCHing into green anacondas to rescue a girl from Charlie's school after she fell into the river.

But all of this pales into insignificance against more Mystery Marble Sender news. We found another marble at the zoo! And there's something about Mystery Marble Sender's note . . . the list of shopping errands on the end . . . that has tickled my memory. The yellow jacket—it's something to do with a yellow jacket. And verrucas . . . I can almost see someone wearing a yellow jacket and tackling their fungal feet . . . but who? Is it my destiny to find out?

Hmmm . . . Destiny . . . Wait. Shhhh! What was that?
Who's there? Josh? Danny?
What?! Hey! What do you think you're—
NO! DOOF! GAH!
Eeeeeeeeeeeeeeeeek.
CRSSHHSZZZZ—kesheeek—ssheeeeek—sheeeek.

Sssssssssssssssssssssssssssssssssssssssssssss
sssssssssssssssssssssssssssssssssssssssssssssss
sssssssssssssssssssssssssssssssssssssssssssssss
sssssssssssssssssssssssssssssssssssssssssssssss
ssssssssssssss

GLOSSARY

Amphibian—An animal that can live on land and in water.

Antidote—Something which takes away the bad effects of a poison or disease.

Cellular—Made of cells.

Constriction—A method used by some snakes to kill their prey. They wrap their bodies around their prey, squeezing it so tight that it cannot breathe.

Hijack—To take control of something by force.

Hologram—A type of photograph made by laser beams, that appears to have depth as well as height and width.

Laboratory—A room or building equipped for scientific work.

Mammal—Any animal of which the female gives birth to live young and can feed them with her own milk.

Prey—An animal that is hunted by another animal for food.

Proximity—To be in the proximity of something is to be near it.

Reptile—A cold-blooded animal. Lizards and snakes are reptiles.

Scales—The thin, overlapping parts on the outside of fish, snakes, and other animals.

Scent—An animal's smell, that other animals can follow.

Serum—A kind of fluid used in science and for medical purposes.

Specimen—An example of one kind of animal, plant, or thing.

Telepathy—Communication of thoughts from one person's mind to another without speaking, writing, or gestures.

Undulating—Moving like a wave or waves.

Venomous—Venom is the poisonous fluid produced by animals such as snakes and scorpions. A venomous snake is poisonous.

PLACES TO VISIT

Want to brush up on your reptile knowledge? Here's a list of places with special areas dedicated to our scaly friends.

New Forest Reptile Centre
http://www.new-forest-national-park.com/new-forest-reptile-centre.html/

London Zoo
http://www.zsl.org/zsl-london-zoo/

Chester Zoo
http://www.chesterzoo.org/animals/reptiles/

WEBSITES

Find out more about nature and wildlife using the websites below.

http://www.nhm.ac.uk/kids-only/

http://kids.nationalgeographic.com/

http://www.switch-books.co.uk/

http://www.arc-trust.org/

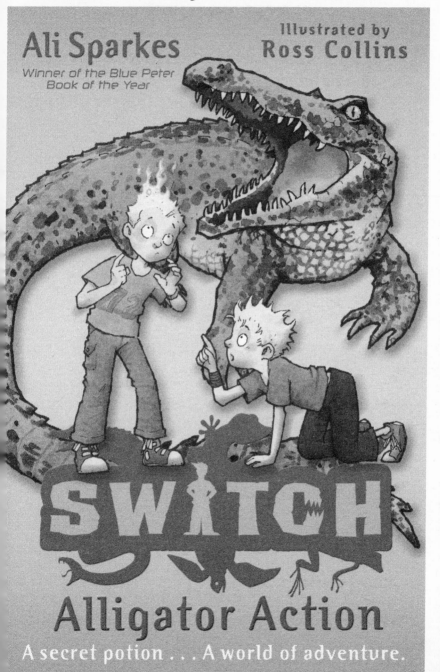

Another exciting adventure awaits . . .

Ali Sparkes

Winner of the Blue Peter
Book of the Year

Illustrated by
Ross Collins

SWITCH
Alligator Action

A secret potion . . . A world of adventure.

Missing Scientist . . .

'Emergency services—which service do you require?'

'Police! Ambulance! Fire and Rescue . . . all of them!' Danny said.

'What is the nature of your emergency?'

'This old lady we know has vanished and we think she's been kidnapped—or killed—or . . . or both!'

'What is your name and address, caller?'

'Eerrrm,' Danny said. 'Well . . . it's kind of secret!'

'Is this a hoax call?'

'NO! It's just that . . . she's a genius scientist who can SWITCH humans into spiders and frogs and snakes and we're her assistants and we have to keep it secret . . . and . . .'

'Young man—hoax calls put other people's lives at risk! If we hear from this number again there will be trouble. I'm hanging up now.'

CLICK. Burrrrrrrrrrrrrrrrrrrrrrrrrrrrrrrrrrrrrrrr.

'That went well, then,' Josh said, who had heard it all on speakerphone. 'I told you it'd be no good! Nobody is going to believe us!'

Danny slumped down in the hallway and hung up the phone with a sigh. Josh was right. How could they ever explain what was really happening? Nobody would believe the truth—that their next-door neighbour was not just a slightly dotty old lady but, in fact, a genius scientist who had developed an amazing SWITCH spray which could turn people into creepy-crawlies and amphibians and reptiles. He and Josh knew it was true—because they *were* the people that Petty had SWITCHed. More times than they could count.

'Come on,' Josh said, peering at the computer print-out in his hand. 'Let's go down to the den. We need to think.'

They walked down the garden and found their way into the rhododendron bush. Piddle, their pet terrier, ran in behind them and sat between Josh and Danny, wagging his tail energetically, hoping for a ball game.

Danny took the computer print-out from his brother and anxiously scratched his spiky blond hair as he read Petty Potts's last diary entry.

When it looked as if Petty still hadn't come back to her house after three days in a row, he and Josh had got so worried they'd gone to check in the car park at Princessland—the girls' toys and frocks superstore over which Petty rented an attic—the location of her new secret laboratory. Petty's old Morris Traveller car had still been there.

So they'd crept through Princessland to the lobby at the back and used the only SWITCH spray they had—Gecko SWITCH—to shrink down to agile lizards and crawl through a gap under the locked door that led to Petty's lab.

And in the lab, as soon as they'd SWITCHed back to boys again, they could see signs of a struggle AND . . . Petty's diary entry still on her computer! She had been speaking her diary into a microphone—using a special program to convert her voice into words on the screen. It was the very last bit which had horrified Josh and Danny.

. . . my SWITCH formula saved a life today! Josh, Danny and Charlie ended up SWITCHing into Green Anacondas to rescue one of the girls from Charlie's school after she fell into the river.

But all of this pales into insignificance against more Mystery Marble Sender news. We found another marble at the zoo! And there's something about Mystery Marble Sender's note . . . the list of shopping errands on the

. . . that has tickled my memory. The yellow jacket—it's something to do with a yellow jacket. And verrucas . . . I can almost see someone wearing a yellow jacket and tackling their fungal feet . . . but who? Is it my destiny to find out?

Hmmm . . . Destiny . . . Wait. Shhhh! What was that?

Who's there? Josh? Danny?

What?! Hey! What do you think you're—

NO! DOOF! GAH!

Eeeeeeeeeeeeeeeeek.

CRSSHHSZZZZ—kesheeek—ssheeeeek—sheeeek.

Ssssssssssssssssssssssssssssssssssssssssssssss
ssssssssssssssssssssssssssssssssssssssssssssss
ssssssssssssssssssssssssssssssssssssssssssssss
ssssssssssssssssssssssssssssssssssssssssssssssss
sssssssss

'What does "CRSSHHSZZZZ—kesheeek—ssheeeeek—sheeeek" mean?' Danny murmured.
'Nothing good,' Josh said.

'Maybe we should just tell Mum and Dad everything when they get back from the shops,' sighed Danny.

'But they'll never believe us, either!' Josh said.

'Not all the stuff about her SWITCHing us into spiders and frogs and snakes and that—just that we think she's in trouble,' Danny said.

'And then what?' Josh said. 'They'll call the police and they'll break into her house—boom—crash—fizz—mangled people! If only Petty wasn't so paranoid about people being out to get her!'

'Yeah,' Danny said. 'But it looks like someone *did* get her.'

Josh and Danny frowned at each other over Piddle's head. They were thinking of the same thing. The Mystery Marble Sender. The person who had been messing with their minds for weeks now—sending clues to get them to find marbles . . . but not just any marbles.

'We knew something *big* was going to happen next, after we got that fifth marble,' Josh said. 'We knew there was only one more to go and the Mystery Marble Sender would soon do something.

Because there was no way he was just giving us clues to find all the marbles, with the secret code to MAMMALSWITCH formula, free. He wants something. And I think it's Petty—or what's in Petty's genius head.'

'Well, if she's been kidnapped,' Danny said, 'I think *we* might get the ransom note. Probably quite soon . . . I mean, there's nobody else to send it to, is there? She's got no family.'

Piddle suddenly got up and tore out of the den, yapping loudly. He ran down the side passage and around to the front of the house. This usually meant somebody was coming in through the gate. Josh and Danny, still worried and gloomy, scrambled out of the bush and went down the side passage to the front to see who was there.

They saw nobody at the gate or the front door—or anywhere around the garden—but Piddle was still flinging himself against the garden wall. Mum and Dad had arrived back, though. Dad was in the kitchen, sorting out the shopping and Mum was watching Chatz TV. The sound of the show drifted out through the front room window. Mum and Jenny liked to watch it most afternoons, although Josh and Danny couldn't imagine *why*. It was mostly people shouting angrily at each other in front of a studio audience. Still, Mum was watching it now and obviously hadn't been interrupted by anyone at the door.

'Shut up, Piddle!' Danny called, and the little dog gave one last disgruntled wuff and then ran back down the side passage. Josh stood very still. Across the low wall he could just make out somebody standing, silently, on Petty's front step.

'Come on,' he said, grabbing Danny's arm and leading him round to Petty's. A dark-haired young woman in a grey suit stood with her back to the door, holding a briefcase. She clearly did not expect anyone to open the door. She smiled tightly at them as they walked up the path.

'You must be Josh and Danny Phillips,' she said.
'I've been waiting for you.'

FUN AND GAMES

There are more games for you to play and download free on the SWITCH website.

www.switch-books.co.uk

Word search

Search for the hidden words listed below:

DANNY
JOSH
PIDDLE
PETTY
ANACONDA
SWITCH

SPRAY
RIVER
CHARLIE
BRIDGE
ADVENTURE
MARBLE

W	B	R	I	D	G	E	R	V	A
C	S	J	C	J	M	Q	I	D	N
N	P	U	X	N	S	C	V	L	A
G	R	E	D	W	H	E	E	P	C
Y	A	Q	T	C	N	E	R	T	O
S	Y	K	T	T	L	H	F	X	N
J	D	I	U	B	Y	N	N	A	D
O	W	R	R	F	O	Z	J	R	A
S	E	A	P	I	D	D	L	E	T
H	M	C	H	A	R	L	I	E	H

Answers on page 124

Spot the difference

These pictures *look* the same,
but can you spot ten differences?

Answers on page 124

True or false?

1. A snake's tongue is shaped liked a spoon.

2. The fastest snake in the world is the black mamba of Africa.

3. Snakes "play dead" to trick their predators.

4. Snakes need feeding every day.

5. Snakes' scales are made from a material quite like our fingernails.

6. Snakes don't have ears.

7. Snakes can't shut their eyes.

8. There are no poisonous snakes in Australia.

9. A snake can swallow an animal larger than its head.

10. When snakes and lizards smell something interesting, their tongues flick in and out very fast.

Answers on page 125

Laugh-out-loud jokes

Q) What's a snake's favourite subject?
A) HISStory!

Q) What's a baby's favourite snake?
A) A rattle snake!

Q) Why was the snake so good at maths?
A) He was an adder!

Q) Why is it impossible to play a trick on a snake?
A) Because you can't pull its leg!

Q) What's long and slimy and found at the North Pole?
A) A lost snake!

Q) What do you call snakes that inform the police?
A) Grass snakes!

Answers

Word search (page 120)

Spot the difference (page 121)

Answers

True or false? (page 122)

1. False—it is shaped like a fork.
2. True—it can reach top speeds of 19kmph
3. True—they lie still with their mouth open and tongue hanging out.
4. False—snakes don't need to eat often and may only eat five or six times a year.
5. True.
6. True—they can't hear anything, but they sense vibrations to know if something's close.
7. True—they don't have eyelids. Snakes' eyes are covered with see-through scales.
8. False—there are more poisonous snakes than non-poisonous ones.
9. True—a snake's jaws are hinged so that they can open very wide.
10. True.

About the author

Ali Sparkes grew up in the wilds of the New Forest, raised by sand lizards who taught her the secret language of reptiles and how to lick her own eyes.

At least, that's how Ali remembers it. Her parents, brother and two sisters argue that she grew up in a council house in Southampton, raised by her mum and dad, who taught her the not terribly secret language of English and wished she'd stop chewing her hair.

She once caught a slow worm and it flicked around like a mad thing and she was a bit scared and dropped it.

Ali still lives in Southampton, now with her husband and two teenage sons, and likes to hang out in the nearby Hawthorn Wildlife Centre spying on common lizards. The lizards are considering legal action . . .

Whether you're interested in insects or revolted by reptiles, you'll love the SWITCH website!

Find out more about the creatures in Josh and Danny's adventures, enter fantastic competitions, read the first chapters of all of the SWITCH books, and enjoy lots of games and activities.

www.switch-books.co.uk